Library of Congress Cataloging in Publication Number: 2019930326

ISBN: 978-1-68369-136-5

Printed in China

Typeset in Clarendon and Gill Sans

Story adapted by Rebecca Gyllenhaal
Production management by John J. McGurk

Quirk Books
215 Church Street
Philadelphia, PA 19106
quirkbooks.com

10 9 8 7 6 5 4 3

HOME ALONE 2
LOST IN NEW YORK

Based on the story written by John Hughes
and directed by Chris Columbus

Illustrated by Kim Smith

QUIRK BOOKS

PHILADELPHIA

'Twas three nights before Christmas, and the McCallister family was getting ready for their vacation to Florida.

Everyone was busy packing.

Everyone except for Kevin, who didn't want to go.

"Why do we have to go to Florida for Christmas?" Kevin asked.
"They have palm trees instead of Christmas trees there!"

"I wish I could go on my own vacation—alone!" Kevin shouted.
"I'd have the best time of my life!" But nobody listened.

They went to the airport the next day. It was crowded and noisy.
Kevin needed to blow his nose, so he borrowed his dad's bag
and stopped to look for a tissue. His family rushed on ahead.

"Wait up!" Kevin yelled, and ran after them.
He thought he could see his dad's coat in the crowd.
He finally caught up to his dad . . .

. . . and boarded the plane
at the very last minute.

When the plane finally landed, Kevin looked out the window.

He saw very tall buildings and lots of snow.
It didn't look like Florida at all.

When Kevin got off the plane, his family was nowhere to be seen!

At first Kevin was scared, but then he realized this was his chance to do whatever he wanted on vacation. He discovered that New York City was a magical place to celebrate Christmas.

He rode around in a yellow cab.

He saw the Statue of Liberty.

He went to the top of
the tallest building,

and he walked through
Central Park.

There was a wallet in his dad's bag, so Kevin checked into the fanciest hotel in the city.

There was no one to tell him what to do, so Kevin watched lots of TV and ate lots of food from room service.

ANGELS WITH EVEN FILTHIER SOULS

The Ventilator

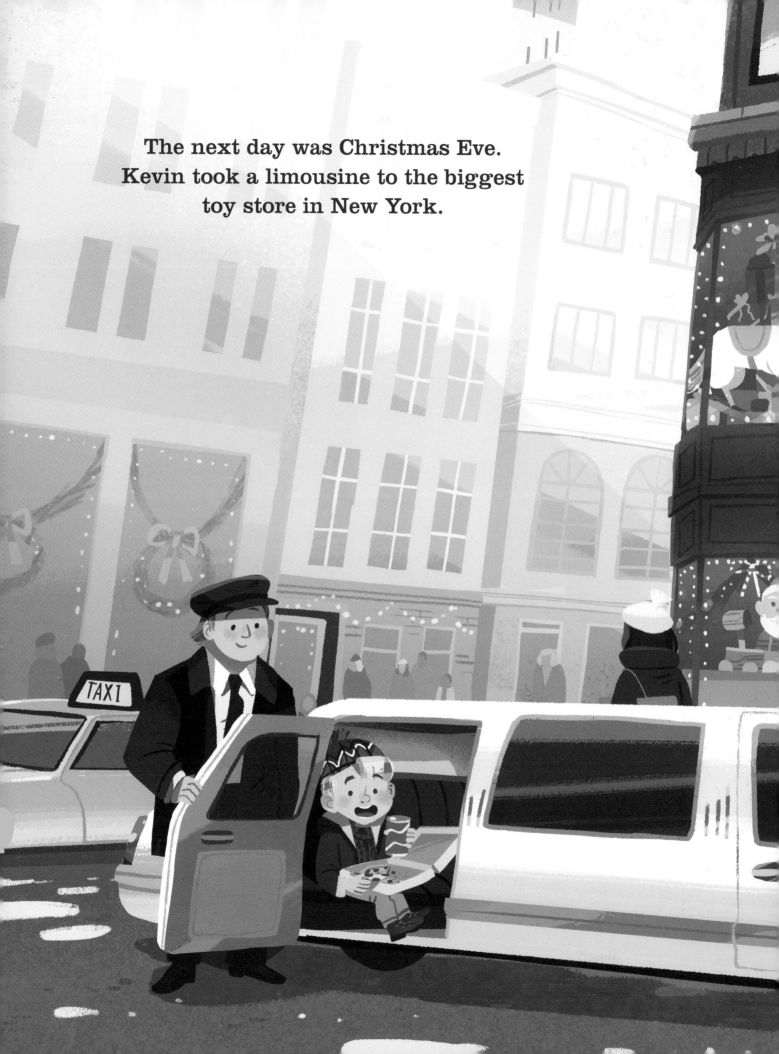

The next day was Christmas Eve.
Kevin took a limousine to the biggest
toy store in New York.

He met the store's owner,
Mr. Duncan, who told Kevin that
all of the money the store earned
on Christmas Eve would be
donated to a children's hospital.

Kevin gave him his whole allowance. He thought the kids in the hospital needed it more than he did. To thank Kevin, Mr. Duncan gave him a pair of special ornaments.

Turtledoves are a symbol of friendship. One dove you should keep, and the other you should give to a true friend.

Kevin left the store and looked at his map for directions.
He wanted to visit the biggest Christmas tree in the city.
Then, someone tapped him on the shoulder.

Kevin turned around . . . and screamed!

It was Harry and Marv, the burglars who tried to rob his house last Christmas Eve, when he was home alone!

Kevin ran away as fast as he could.
He ran all the way across Central Park.

He ran so fast that he tripped,
and his foot got caught
between two rocks.

A woman approached. She was covered in birds. Kevin was scared at first, but then she pulled his foot free of the rocks.

The bird lady told Kevin that she lived in the park and that the pigeons were her only friends. She was spending Christmas without her family, just like Kevin.

Kevin thanked her for helping him and promised that he would come back to visit her.

But first, Kevin had to stop the burglars from robbing the toy store.

At an abandoned house nearby, he made a plan.

Kevin poured goo on the floor,

and tied paint cans to ropes,

and lined up bags of flour.

He stretched a trip wire
across the basement,

and scattered tools
in the hallway,

and painted the
stairs with grease.

Kevin went back to the toy store.
Harry and Marv were already there,
stuffing money into a bag.

The burglars chased Kevin to the abandoned house.

Then, they stumbled into all of Kevin's traps.

Marv and Harry tripped on the tools in the hallway . . .

. . . and slipped down the stairs
that were painted with grease.

But as Kevin
snuck away,
the burglars
spotted him.

They chased after him
and dragged him back
to Central Park.

Suddenly, the bird lady appeared and threw birdseed all over Harry and Marv, who were covered in goo.

The pigeons swarmed Harry and Marv and pecked at them until the police arrived.

It was almost midnight, which meant that it was almost Christmas. Kevin went to look at the biggest Christmas tree in New York City. He missed his family. It turned out that going on vacation alone wasn't much fun after all.

And then he heard a familiar voice.

Kevin turned around . . . and there was his mom!

She knew Kevin better than anyone, so she remembered how much he loved Christmas trees. She knew exactly where to find him.

Kevin's whole family was waiting back at the hotel.

"I missed you all so much," Kevin said.

On Christmas morning, a giant pile of presents sat under the tree. They were all from Mr. Duncan, who left a note thanking Kevin for saving his toy store. But as his brothers and sisters opened their gifts, Kevin quietly slipped away.

There was someone he wanted to see.

Kevin hadn't forgotten the bird lady who helped him so much.
He gave her the other turtledove ornament, which meant
they would be friends forever.

All was peaceful . . . until his dad yelled so loudly that Kevin could hear him from the park.

KEVIN! You spent 967 dollars on room service?!